I0829495

Light Touch Art
Presents

By

Judi Light

Creator of the Twigshire Books

Published by
Light Touch Art ™
Venice, Florida
and
Heritage Publishing.US
Bradenton, Florida

DEDICATION

This book is dedicated to the

Wonderful Wee Wishers in the World.

It all begins with you!

... you were a bug,
Would you live on a plant?
Would you sit on the leaf of a flower
In your pants
If you were a bug ...

Would you?

... you were a bird

Would you live in a tree?

Would you visit your friends and
drink mulberry tea

If you were a bird ...

Would You?

... you were a snail
Would you live in the grass?
Would you eat all the weeds
As you slowly moved past
If you were a snail...

Would you?

... you were a mouse
Would you live in some hay?
Would you tickle your friend
Pull her whiskers in play
If you were a mouse...

Would you?

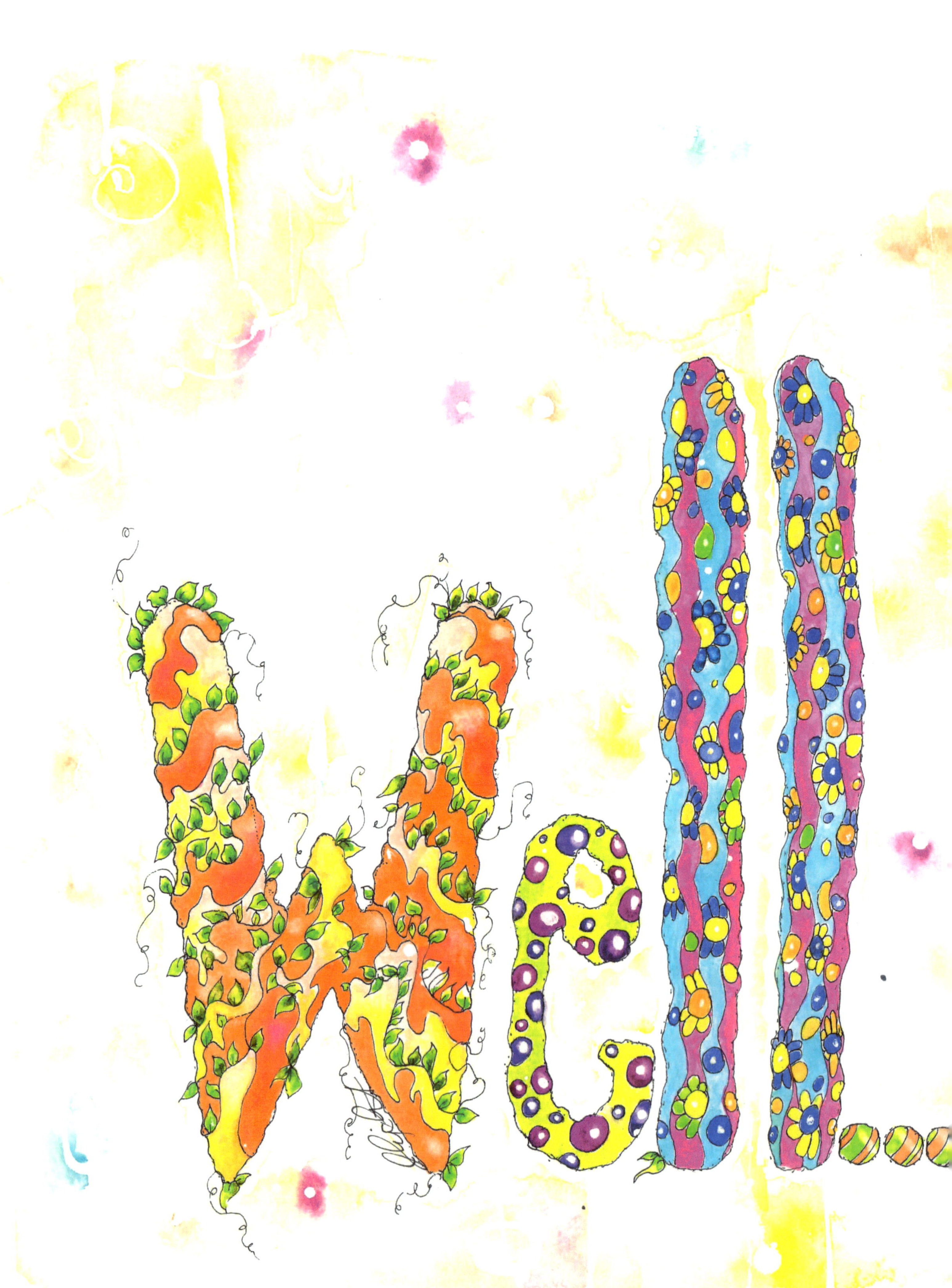
Well...

... I'm not a bug
Or a bird
Snail or mouse.
I don't live in a tree...

I live in a house-just
like you!

my House

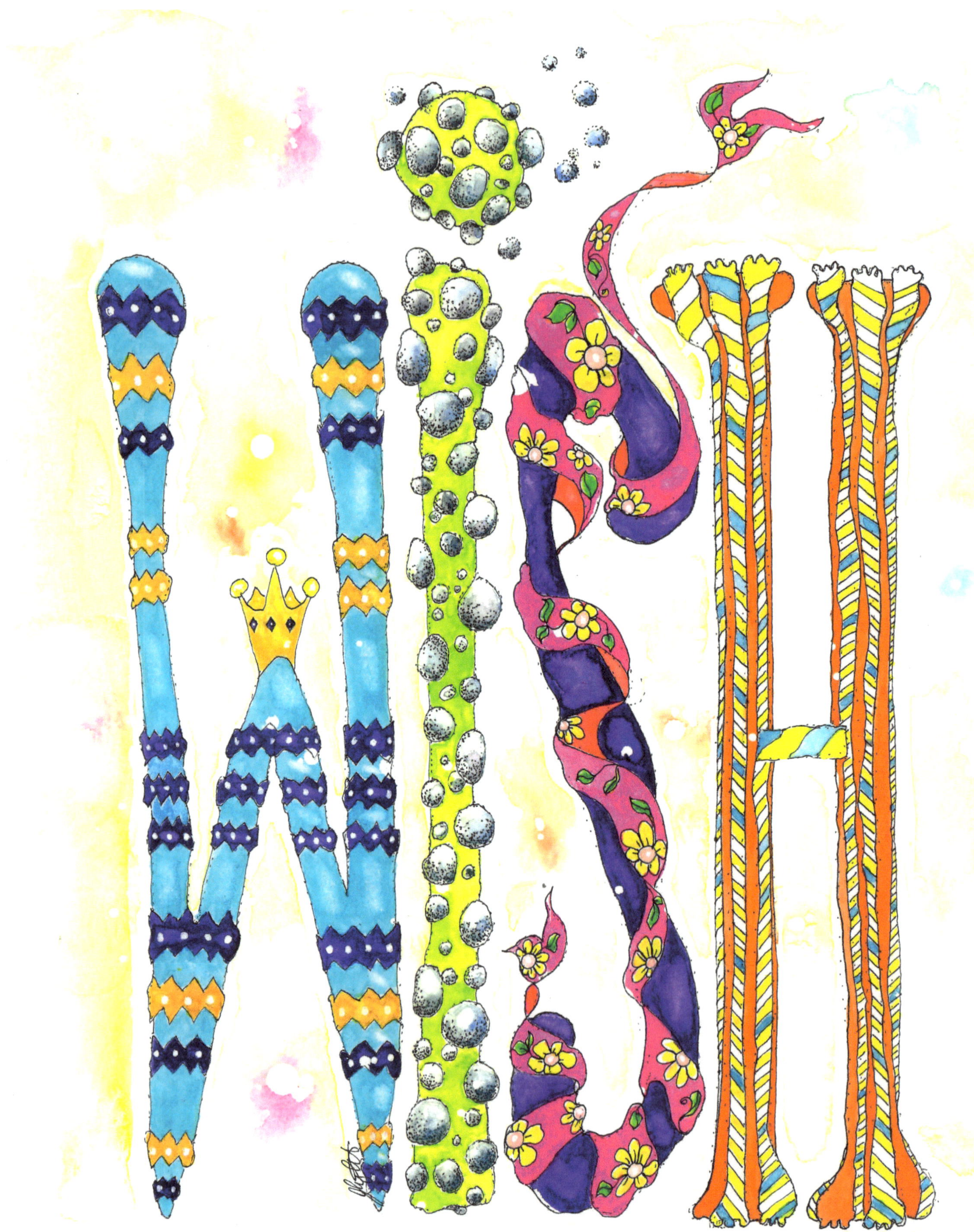

Sometimes I WISH

I could live in a tree,

I'll pretend for a bit that the bug's really me,

Or I think I can play hide and seek in the hay

Or glide through the grass til the end of the day.

... I'm just a small person
(I'm older than three)
And wishing these wishes is what makes me

Me!

Acknowledgements

I'd like to thank Brenda Spalding of Braden River Consulting for helping me with all of the layout, text design and general hand holding needed to get this wee book done!

You truly came to my rescue!

To Mary Lee, Curator and Founder of the Marietta Museum of Art and Whimsy, who has encouraged, befriended ,supported and given me many good ideas along the way. Her initial belief in me and my art allowed for the creation of my last three books.

Thank you to ALL my Twigshire and Light Touch Art fans big and small.

You are my reason for painting and writing. I appreciate and love every one of you.

The Artist and Author

JUDI LIGHT is British born, Canadian raised and after living abroad and in many cities in the U.S. now resides in Venice, Florida.

In 2011, after years away from her art, she revisited her black and white Wee Folk characters, (who were patiently awaiting her return) with the added bonus of discovering the total joy of watercolor. That's when the Magic happened!

 Whimsical paintings and stories began arriving, along with the wonderful township of Twigshire!!

Her use of fine tipped engineering pens with which she creates images using thousands of dots, then painting many layers of watercolor washes, results in very detailed images alive with color and depth.

Many of her original watercolors now reside in the permanent collection of the well known Marietta Museum of Art and Whimsy in Sarasota, Florida. All are welcome at the Whimsy Museum to experience and enjoy a fabulous world of art.

 Judi says that "... the purpose of my art and books is to ramp up the Happiness Factor, possibly encourage some insight, perhaps impart a life lesson...and ALWAYS to leave you smiling."

Judi has also illustrated and authored four Magical World of Twigshire Books which are available through her website **www.LightTouchArt.com** or from the Cottage Gallery, in Nokomis Florida, where her work is displayed and where she is the curator for over 20 local artists.

Light Touch Art
The Magical World of Twigshire

"Ms. Light's illustrations are glorious; vibrant, highly detailed and so beautifully drawn that you can look at them forever and still keep seeing more.

The whole book is absolutely charming; loaded with touches of magic and sweet little messages about feeling good inside. Beautifully written. Utter magic.(5 Stars!)"

Amelia Curzon, UK Children's Book Author and Reviewer.

"Wow! Judi Light's artwork and poetry do just what her name suggests: she brings light and laughter to the world of literature. Her artwork is magical."

Dr. Laura KIngsley, School Principal, Sarasota, Fl

"Judi Light's book takes you to a world full of enchantment. Her Twigshire series is an absolute joy, not just for children but for the child in everyone. In her third book she introduces us to the charms of the underwater world of Blue Bottom Bay. Beautifully illustrated and delightfully written, the Twigshire characters find a way into our hearts to warm them!"

Kristy Reeves, Writer/Actor, Founder/Producer of TheChildrenoftheRainbow.org documentary series.

"The Magical world of Twigshire series is a beautiful treasure, delight for the senses and accessible to all ages. As an educator, I use them in my classes to encourage reflection and spark creativity.

 I highly recommend the read and mental journey you will embark upon to uncharted shores".

Steffanie Grotz, Inverness Middle School, Teacher of the Gifted and 8th Grade Adv. E.L.A.